# THIS BLOOMSBURY BOOK

## BELONGS TO

...........................................................

For Mum, Dad,
Max, Indi and kit.

Bloomsbury Publishing, London, Berlin and New York

First published in Great Britain in 2003 by Bloomsbury Publishing Plc
36 Soho Square, London, W1D 3QY

This paperback edition first published in June 2004

Text and illustrations copyright © Natalie Russell 2003
The moral right of the author/illustrator has been asserted

A CIP catalogue record of this book is available from the British Library

ISBN 978 0 7475 6486 7

Printed in Belgium by Proost,Turnhout

10

All papers used by Bloomsbury Publishing are natural,
recyclable products made from wood grown in well-managed forests.
The manufacturing processes conform to the environmental regulations
of the country of origin.

www.bloomsbury.com

# Hamish
## the Highland Cow

## by Natalie Russell

BLOOMSBURY

LONDON  BERLIN  NEW YORK

It was springtime in the glen.
All the animals were preening
and cleaning their spring coats.

# Hamish, the Highland Cow!

Hamish NEVER groomed
his long tangly coat,
he HATED having baths
and he certainly NEVER
EVER let anyone cut
his hair.

Hamish's hair was so **LONG** that he couldn't always see through it.

It was so KNOTTY and TANGLY that THINGS lived in it.

And it was so STICKY with toffee that EVERYTHING stuck to it.

You see, Hamish **LOVED** eating toffee — sticky, gooey, chewy toffee. And the perfect place to keep his toffee treats was in his long tangly coat.

But the other animals had had enough of Hamish's stinky, dirty, matted hair.

PONG!

POO-WEE

PONG!

"It's time you had a haircut, Hamish," said Cat.

"What?" cried Hamish. "A haircut ... NEVER!"

"We'll give you a big surprise!" said Rabbit.

NOW Hamish LOVED surprises.

"Hmmm," he thought, "what if the surprise was a never-ending supply of toffee?" "Mmm, maybe a wee trim," he said to his friends.

So the next morning the animals and a very
nervous Hamish set off for the hairdresser.

It wasn't far and before long they had arrived.
Hamish slowly peered around the salon door.

# What a sight!

There were

pink sheep,

blue sheep,

stripy sheep,

and polka-dot sheep.

There were sheep with
big hair, short hair,
long hair and
curly-wurly hair.

SHEEP CHIC

And there, in the middle of them all,
snipping and clipping away was

# THE HAIRDRESSER!

Hamish hadn't realised that the hairdresser could be so much fun. There were lots of books to read.

RECIPES

SWEETIES

MMM

And great things to play with...

SNIFF

SNIFF

Smelly things...

"Mr Hamish," said the hairdresser.
"What will it be today, sir?"

Hamish still felt a bit nervous
but he took a deep breath...
"A w-w-wee trim, p-p-please," he said.

The hairdresser set to work on Hamish's coat.

IT SMELLS OUT HERE!

POO-WEE

With a snippety-snip and a clippety-clip the scissors whizzed over Hamish's long tangly coat.

It didn't hurt at all. "What do you think, Mr Hamish?" asked the hairdresser.

Hamish looked in the mirror...

"GROOVY!" he beamed.

ALL the animals agreed. And the hairdresser even gave Hamish Lots of toffees for being so brave.

But Hamish Looked sad.
"I've got nowhere to keep them," he said.

SHHH!

SHHHHH!

THEN,

"**SURPRISE!**" shouted his friends.

And they gave Hamish a very special bag to put all his yummy toffees in.

Hamish was delighted.
He popped his toffees in his bag
and set off home with his friends.

"Now you're the coolest cow in the Highlands," said the animals, giving Hamish a huge hug. "Don't mess up my hair!" said a very smart and sweet-smelling Hamish.

# ENJOY MORE GREAT PICTURE BOOKS FROM BLOOMSBURY ...

**THE GOSSIPY PARROT**
Shen Roddie & Michael Terry

**GOODNIGHT LULU**
Paulette Bogan

**BRUNA**
Anne Cottringer & Gillian McClure

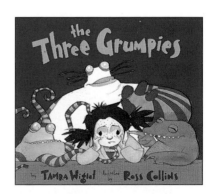

**THE THREE GRUMPIES**
Tamra Wight & Ross Collins